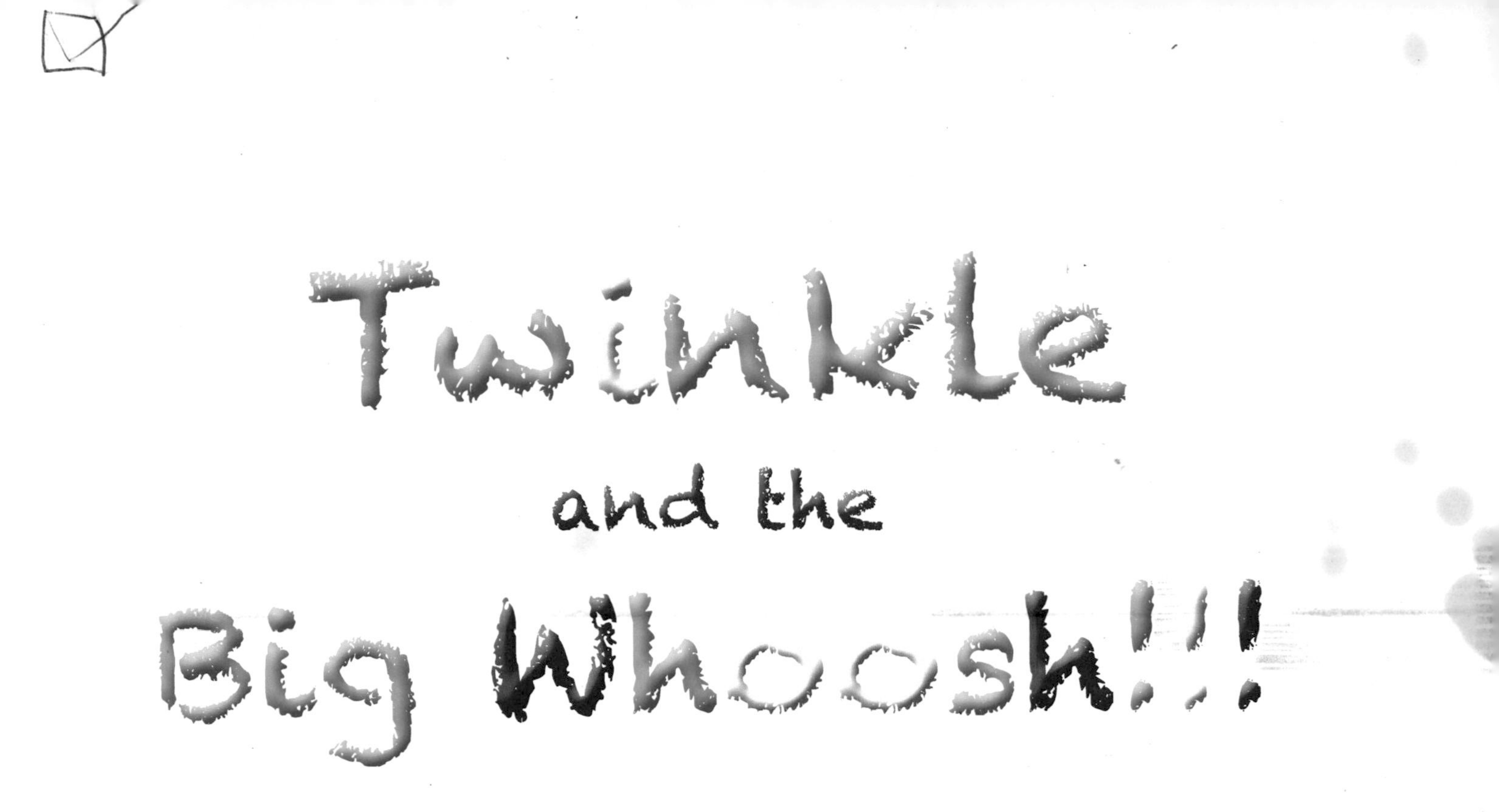

Twinkle and the Big Whoosh!!!

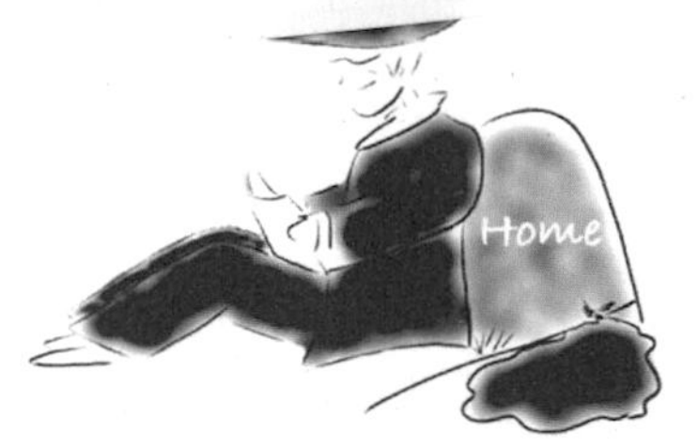

Tatterdemalion Blue

First published by **Tatterdemalion** Blue in 2014

A CIP catalogue record for this book is available from the British Library

Cover design and layout by **Tatterdemalion** Blue

ISBN 978-0-9573315-4-9

Tatterdemalion Blue
8 Upper Bridge Street
Stirling
FK8 1ER

www.tatterdemalionblue.com

Twinkle and the Big Whoosh!!!

Written by ~ Angela Mair
Illustrated by ~ Jeremy Wyatt

... for my lovely grandchildren ...

Jamie - Poppy - Oscar - Sophie

and Forbes

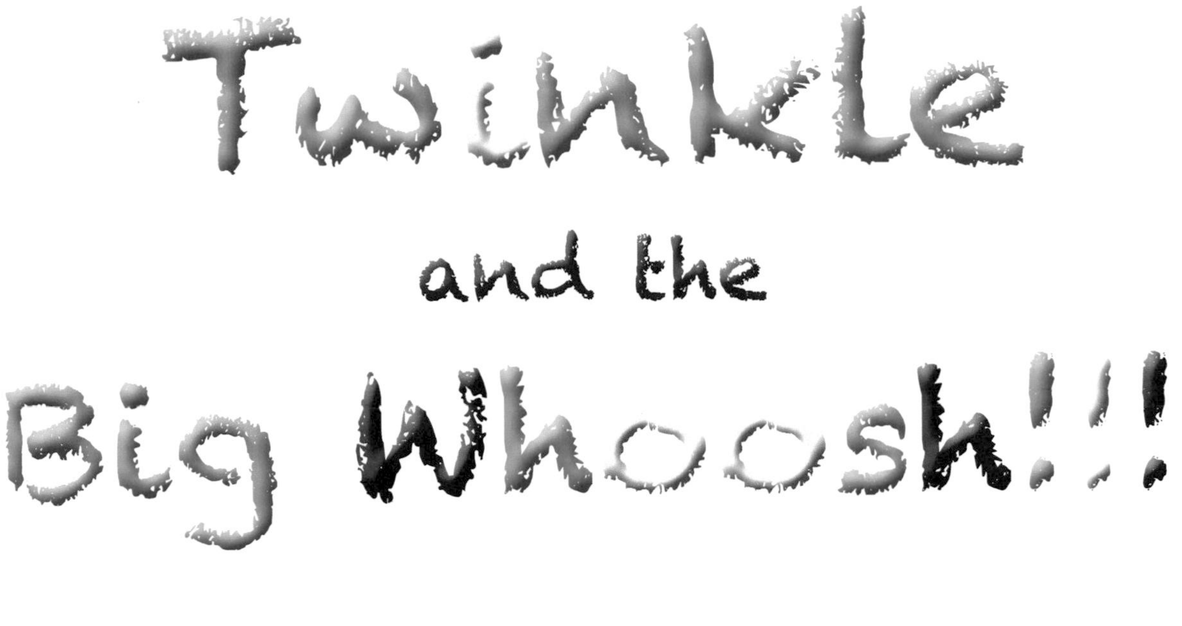
Twinkle
and the
Big Whoosh!!!

One winter's night in December
a little baby Star was born.
She was tiny,
just a twinkle
and Twinkle is her name.
Being born close to Christmas
was seen as a special honour indeed
and so great was the joy of all the other stars
that they filled the heavens with stardust.
The Skies became so bright and shiny
that the people on Earth looking up
had to shield their eyes from the light.

She was a very happy little Star but she was growing up fast. Soon it would be time for her to go to school and join all the other Twinklers.

Twinklers was the name given to young Stars when they went to the great Sky School.

Twinkle had to learn many new things at school, like how to stay very still for a long, long time, which was difficult for a young Star. She also had to learn how to be very quiet, which was also very hard to do as she found everything so exciting.

Best of all, Twinkle had to learn how to shine brightly. This was so easy and so much fun too. All she had to do was to think of something happy that made her smile, and immediately she lit up and she shone and shone. She was a very good student and learned her lessons well. She became excellent at being very quiet and very, very still.

The most difficult thing was yet to come.

All the little Twinklers were talking about it and whispers and mutterings could be heard in the class. Twinkle and all the other students would have to learn how to fly the Big Whoosh across the Skies.

"Hmmm!" said the Master of the Skies, "no chattering in the ranks please."

Twinkle had a big problem. She was scared that she would not be able to fly the Big Whoosh across the midnight Skies. She was so small compared to all the others. Oh dear! What was she going to do?

She was afraid of heights. It seemed so dangerous for a young Star to fly the Big Whoosh to become a Shooting Star like the grown ups. But it had to done. She shivered with fear and tried to hide in the line of the other excited Twinklers.

The Master of the Skies saw her trying to hide and called out her name. It was no good, she would have to take her turn. Twinkle stood at the front of the line, feeling so tiny against the dark Night Sky.

"Come on Twinkle, you can do it," shouted her classmates, encouraging her as much as they could. "Remember to think happy thoughts to help you to fly."

Her eyes were closed as she took a deep breath and pushed herself out into the dark Skies. She could feel the cool wind blowing against her cheeks, but she kept her eyes tightly shut and began to feel afraid. All of a sudden, she was tumbling and falling, and falling and tumbling.

"Oh no!" she cried out, thinking she would fall all the way to the hard Earth. Instead, she felt a cushioned bump and a soggy splash! She opened her eyes to see two large dark grey eyes staring back at her.

"Who are you?" Twinkle asked.

Two sad eyes looked at her and said, "I am Fluffy. I am a baby Cloud and I am lost. You fell onto to me."

"Who are you?" asked Fluffy.

"I am Twinkle and I was doing my first Big Whoosh across the Sky."

"Oh," said the baby Cloud. "I am very pleased to meet you, but I am very unhappy. I can't find my Mummy. We were out floating and there was a lot of other clouds, but I got lost. I am very sad."

"Oh dear," said Twinkle, "don't worry, I will help you to look for your Mummy. I am sure we will find her."

Twinkle turned around and around looking for the Mother Cloud when suddenly there came a big cry from above and a large Mummy Cloud came racing across the Skies to meet them.

Fluffy saw his Mummy and began to cry and as he sobbed Twinkle started to slip down through the damp Cloud. You see, the little Cloud's tears were rain and they were sliding down his sides. Twinkle was slipping with the rain drops and she could not hold on.

Finally she fell right through the little Cloud and was again falling and tumbling through the Skies with her eyes tight shut. Down and down she fell when suddenly, she was not falling anymore but being blown in circles, side to side, across the Night Sky. Twinkle heard a laugh, and then another, as she was being blown around and around. It was starting to make her feel a bit dizzy.

"Stop!" shouted Twinkle.

Suddenly she stopped still. She opened her eyes but there was nothing or no one to see. Only giggling and laughter could be heard.

"Who are you?" Twinkle asked, a little scared.

"I am Buzz, a baby Whirlwind," said the laughing voice, "and I am learning how to be a Big Twister."

"Oh," said Twinkle, "well you had better take me back to my school."

"Oh no," said Buzz, "I can't do that. I can only twist sideways."

More giggling was heard and Twinkle began to spin round and round with the baby Twister. Just as Twinkle was about to be sick with the dizzy spinning, she felt herself stop. She was not going round and round anymore.

The naughty little Whirlwind had dropped her. All she could hear was Buzz giggling and laughing. Again Twinkle was falling and tumbling, down and down. She closed her eyes tight shut once more, listening to the giggling and laughter fading away into the distance.

Suddenly Twinkle felt a soft bump and found herself bouncing up and down. What had she fallen onto this time? Twinkle, feeling a little scared, opened her eyes and saw she was surrounded by fluffy white feathers.

"Oh my, where am I?" she spluttered, spitting the fluffy white feathers from her mouth.

"You are on my back dear," a kindly voice said, "I am a Mother Goose. My name is Flora."

She had fallen onto the back of a high flying Goose.

"Are you lost little Star?"

"Yes I am. I was at school ready to attempt the Big Whoosh when I fell, and now here I am."

"That sounds exciting," said Flora, "but don't worry dear, you will soon find your way home, I am sure."

It was a lovely comfortable place to land, just like a bouncy bed. Twinkle bounced and bounced, it was such fun.

"Do you like my feathery back?" asked the Mother Goose.

"Oh, I am so sorry," Twinkle said. "I hope I didn't hurt you."

"No, not a bit my dear, you are so light."

"Where are you going?" asked Twinkle.

"I am going to the Grazing Grounds where there is lots of food for me to eat. All my family will be there too."

"Are you going to Earth?" said Twinkle, panicking.

"Yes," said Flora, "I am."

"I cannot go with you Flora. I am just a little Star and I can never fall to Earth as I would break."

"Oh my," said Flora, "you will have to leave me, but first, let me help."

She flew as high as she could, spread her wings wide and tilted over, allowing Twinkle to slide off her soft feathery back.

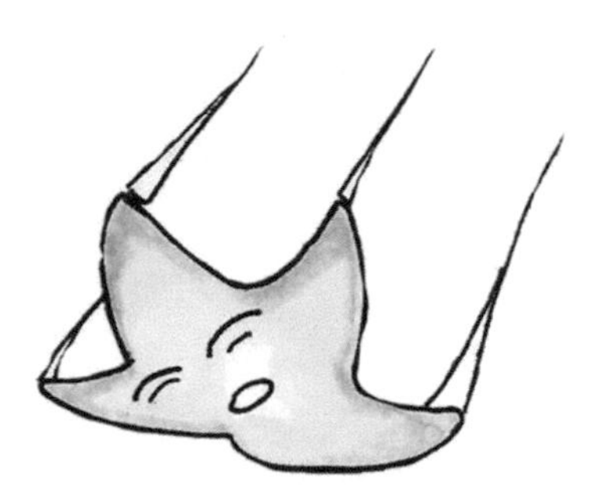

"Goodbye Flora," shouted Twinkle.

"Goodbye dear," called Flora.

Twinkle could hear the soft swish of the Mother Goose's large feathery wings. Once again she started to fall.

Oh no! Twinkle was falling and falling, faster and faster, down and down when suddenly and thankfully she felt herself floating upwards. What was happening? Twinkle opened her eyes and saw that she was being gently cradled in the arms of her kind Mother Star, who had been carefully watching over her all along.

The Mother Star flew Twinkle back to her friends at the school. They all gathered round and gave her a big hug. Twinkle told them all about her adventure. How she had fallen into Fluffy, the baby Cloud, who was lost. But then he found his mother. Then she told them of the cheeky laughing baby Twister, Buzz, who made her so dizzy.

Finally, she told them about Flora, the lovely Mother Goose, who had helped her when she fell onto her feathery back.

The Master of the Skies said that she had been a very brave little Star indeed, and she was given a lovely golden smile sticker. All of her little Star friends were so pleased to have her back that they all started to shine brightly.

Twinkle felt so proud. She could not help smiling and laughing, and as she did so something wonderful happened. She started to shine and shine until she shone so brightly that she puffed up and shot out across the skies, sprinkling stardust far behind her.

The Big Whoosh!!!

All the Stars cheered.

The Night Skies were ablaze with the happiness of all the Shooting Stars, shining and sprinkling stardust as each in turn whooshed across the heavens.

Looking up, the Mother Cloud and Fluffy smiled in wonder at the little Star.

Laughing and giggling, Buzz, the baby Twister, spun around, blowing her a kiss.

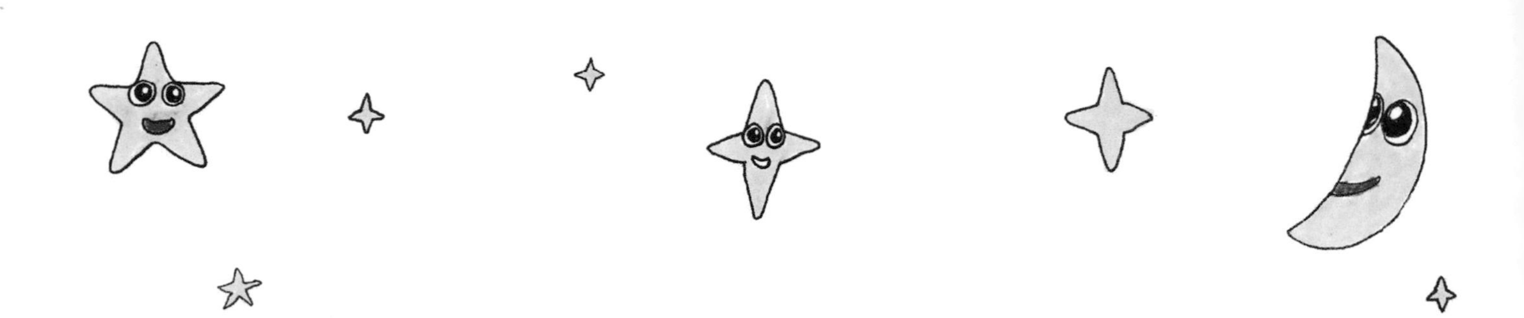

Flora, the Mother Goose, and all her family and friends watched happily from the Grazing Grounds. They flapped their wings in joy and happiness at the sight of the little Star sprinkling her stardust across the Skies.

Oh, what an amazing sight to see on a dark December night just before Christmas. And how a tiny Star, with a little help from her family and friends, had overcome her fears.

Twinkle was now truly a Shooting Star.

Lightning Source UK Ltd.
Milton Keynes UK
UKIC01n0909230715
255685UK00010B/55

* 9 7 8 0 9 5 7 3 3 1 5 4 9 *